Sam aı

Teaching Notes

This book contains the following vowels:
a i o u.

This book contains the following consonants:
b d f g h l m n p r s t

This book contains the following non-phonetic sight words:
a do for is no the this was

Prior to Reading:

Look at the cover picture with your child. Ask, "What do you think this book might be about?" Tell them, "The children's names are Sam and Pam," as you point at the title.

While Reading:

Encourage your child to use finger-point reading to track the words across the page. Give them time to decode the word. Avoid jumping in to help too early. If your child gets stuck on a word, prompt them to look at the initial sound of the word and to use the picture for clues. Then sound out the letters with them, scaffolding them to run the sounds together.

After Reading:

Talk about the story. Link the book with their prior knowledge. What made Pam sad? Why did Pam hit Sam? What did Sam do to make Pam feel happy again? Revisit their prediction about what the book was about. Was their prediction correct? Have you ever got angry with a friend? What did you do?

This is Sam. This is Pam.

Sam and Pam had fun.

Sam sat on the bed.

Pam sat on the rug.

Sam ran.

Pam ran.

Sam hid from Pam
in the hut.

Pam was sad.

Sam got a top.

Pam did not get a top.

Pam got mad.

Pam hit Sam on the lip.

"No, Pam, no.
Do not hit Sam."

Sam got a top for Pam.

Sam and Pam had a hug.

Sam and Pam
sat on the rug.

Sam and Pam had fun.

The end.

About this book

This book is part of a series of five phonemic early readers. This pink series goes with the pink language materials in a Montessori classroom. The other books in this series will provide reading experiences with more CVC words, short vowel sounds, consonants and sight words.

Other titles in this series are:
- The Rat Ran.
- Can Pig Nap?
- Bad Dog
- The Sun was Hot

Once your child has mastered the pink materials and readers, introduce them to the blue language materials and the five blue phonemic early readers. These will provide reading experiences with longer phonemic words using the same vowel sounds and consonants.

The green series of phonemic readers will provide reading experiences with phonograms, blends and digraphs. They are designed to be introduced when your child has learned the relevant phonograms by using the green language materials.

From the Author

My name is Cath King. I'm a Montessori Teacher in New Zealand. I hope you enjoyed this Pink Reader, and that it has helped you practice reading CVC words. If you enjoyed this book, please leave a review on Amazon. I read every review and they help new readers discover my books.

Get your free printable download of the Pink Reader Word Searches
https://edu-king.weebly.com/download-pink-reader-word-search.html

47396291R00015